Mrs Vole the Vet

Ahlberg & Chichester Clark

PUFFIN

PUFFIN BOOKS
Published by the Penguin Group: London, New York, Australia,
Canada, India, Ireland, New Zealand and South Africa
Penguin Books Ltd, Registered Offices:
80 Strand, London WC2R 0RL, England

puffinbooks.com

First published by Viking 1996
Published by Puffin Books 1996
Published in this edition 2014
001
Text copyright © Allan Ahlberg, 1996
Illustrations copyright © Emma Chichester Clark, 1996
All rights reserved
Educational Advisory Editor: Brian Thompson
The moral right of the author and illustrator has been asserted
Printed and bound in China
ISBN: 978–0–723–29394–1

Meet Mrs Vole the vet.
Mrs Vole has one son,
two daughters,
three cats,
four dogs
and *no* husband.

Mr Vole has three stepsons,
eleven rabbits
and a new wife.
We will forget about him.

Mrs Vole works hard.

She works day and night,

week after week

and all the year round.

No job is too little.

No job is too big.

No job is too fast,

too slow,

or too low.

. . . high.

No job is too . . .

Mrs Vole is worn out.
She comes home from work
and falls asleep in a chair.

Her children make the tea,
put her slippers on –
and worry about her.

"What you need is a *boyfriend*, Mum," they say.

"Hm," says Mrs Vole.

She sips her tea. "Do you think so?"

"Yes!"

"What sort of boyfriend?"

"A nice one!" the children yell.

"With a nice smile!"

"A nice wallet!"

"And nice football boots!"

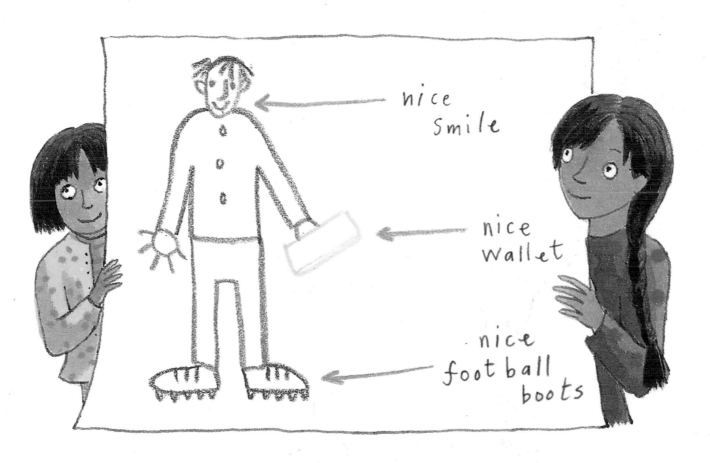

And Mrs Vole thinks, "Hm."

A few days later, Mrs Vole meets
Mr Lamp the lighthouse keeper.

Mr Lamp has a nice smile,
a nice cat
and a nice lighthouse.

"He's not bad, Mum," the children say.
"Hm," says Mrs Vole.
She sips her tea. "The only trouble is . . .

... TOO MANY STEPS!"

"OK," the children say.
"We will forget about him."

A few days later, Mrs Vole meets
Mr Field the farmer.

Mr Field has a nice smile, a nice truck,

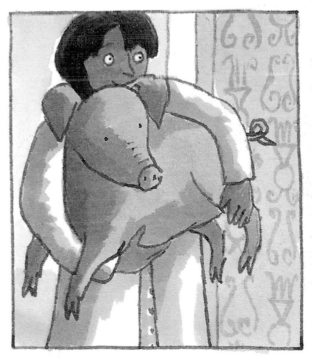

a very nice cheque book and a poorly pig.

"*He's* not bad, Mum," the children say.
"Hm," says Mrs Vole.
"Do you think so?"
"Yes!"

"Lovely cheque book!"
"Lovely pig!"
"Hm," says Mrs Vole.
She sips her tea. "The only trouble is . . .

...A HUNDRED AND FIFTY OTHER PIGS!"

"Phew!" the children say.
"We will forget about *him*."

Mrs Vole goes back to work.
She works seven days a week.
She works seven nights a week.

No job is too big.   No job is too little.

No job is too wet,   too spotty,

BUM!

or too complicated.   No job is too rude.

Mrs Vole is worn out.
She comes home from work
and falls asleep at the table.
Her children make the breakfast,
put her slippers on –
and worry about her.

"What you *really* need
is a boyfriend, Mum," they say.
"Hm," says Mrs Vole.
She eats her cornflakes.
"Do you think so?"

A few weeks later, Mrs Vole meets:

Mr Shout the sergeant.
"Too bossy!"

Mr Green the grocer.
"Too cabbagy!"

Mr Aaargh! the actor.
"Too embarrassing!"

Aaargh!

"OK," the children say.
"We will forget about *them*."

Then, one morning the doorbell rings.
On the step stands a man
in a nice white coat.
He has a nice smile on his face
and a poorly pigeon in his hands.

Meet Mr Moo the milkman.
"Hallo, there!"

Mrs Vole takes care of the pigeon.
The children take care of the milkman.

When Mr Moo leaves,
the children rush up to their mum.
"*He's* not bad, Mum."
"Do you think so?"
"Yes!" the children yell.
"No steps!"
"No pigs!"
"No shouting!"
"You might be right," says Mrs Vole.
"The only trouble is . . .

. . . MRS MOO!"

A few days later,
Mrs Vole and the children
make a picnic
and drive off to the seaside.

The sun is shining.
The sand is warm.
The waves are splashing on the rocks.

Mrs Vole is smiling
as she climbs the *lighthouse* stairs.

"After all," she thinks.
"What's a few steps . . .

. . . between friends."

The End

Plus

Animal Offspring

Tigers and Their Cubs

Revised Edition

Margaret Hall

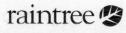

raintree

a Capstone company — publishers for children

Raintree is an imprint of Capstone Global Library Limited, a company incorporated in England and Wales having its registered office at 264 Banbury Road, Oxford, OX2 7DY – Registered company number: 6695582

www.raintree.co.uk
myorders@raintree.co.uk

ISBN 978 1 4747 5630 3 (hardback)
22 21 20 19 18
10 9 8 7 6 5 4 3 2 1

ISBN 978 1 4747 5640 2 (paperback)
23 22 21 20 19
10 9 8 7 6 5 4 3 2 1

British Library Cataloging in Publication Data
A full catalogue record for this book is available from the British Library.

Editorial Credits
Gina Kammer, editor; Sarah Bennett, designer; Morgan Walters, media researcher; Katy LaVigne, production specialist

Printed and bound in India

Acknowledgements
We would like to thank the following for permission to reproduce photographs:
Getty Images: CHARLY TRIBALLEAU, 9; Shutterstock: Africa Studio, 13, Anan Kaewkhammul, 11, left 20, chanyut Sribua-rawd, right 20, Cynthia Kidwell, Cover, Dennis Jacobsen, 5, George Lamson, 15, Julian W, 17, neelsky, right 21, otsphoto, left 21, Raj Wildberry, 1, Volodymyr Burdiak, 19, Xseon, 7

Every effort has been made to contact copyright holders of material reproduced in this book. Any omissions will be rectified in subsequent printings if notice is given to the publisher.

All the Internet addresses (URLs) given in this book were valid at the time of going to press. However, due to the dynamic nature of the Internet, some addresses may have changed, or sites may have changed or ceased to exist since publication. While the author and publisher regret any inconvenience this may cause readers, no responsibility for any such changes can be accepted by either the author or the publisher.

Contents

Tigers

Tigers are mammals.

Tigers are large cats
with whiskers.

A female is a tigress.

Young tigers are cubs.

A male tiger mates

with a tigress.

The male tiger leaves

before the cubs are born.

Tiger cubs

A tigress gives birth to two

or three cubs.

The cubs drink milk

from her body.

Cubs are born blind and deaf.

They can see and

hear after two weeks.

Growing up

Cubs rest during the day.

They grow quickly.

The tigress licks the cubs

to clean them.

She keeps them safe.

The tigress teaches the cubs
to hunt and find food.

Cubs live with their mothers

for about two years.

Then each cub leaves

to find its own home.

Watch tigers grow

birth

20

adult after
about four years

Glossary

birth to be born; a tigress gives birth to a group of cubs

blind unable to see; tiger cubs are born with their eyes closed; their eyes open after two weeks

deaf unable to hear; cubs can hear after two weeks

mammal warm-blooded animal that has a backbone and hair or fur; female mammals feed milk to their young

mate join together to produce young

tigress adult female tiger

whisker one of the long, stiff hairs near the mouth of an animal

Find out more

Books
Lion vs Tiger (Animal Rivals), Isabel Thomas (Raintree, 2017)

Tiger (Eye on the Wild), Suzi Eszterhas (Frances Lincoln Ltd, 2015)

Tigers (Predator Profile), Julia Vogel (Raintree, 2015)

Websites
www.dkfindout.com/us/animals-and-nature/cats/tiger/
DK Find Out!

www.natgeokids.com/uk/discover/animals/general-animals/10-tiger-facts/.
National Geographic

Comprehension questions

1. Why do the cubs need to learn to hunt?

2. Tigers are mammals. What does the word "mammal" mean?

3. Why is it important for the mother to care for her cubs before they are two weeks old?

Index